DIARY OF A
Big Bad
Wolf

More magical adventures
from Ben Miller:

The Night I Met Father Christmas
The Boy Who Made the World Disappear
The Day I Fell into A Fairytale
How I Became a Dog Called Midnight
The Night We Got Stuck in a Story
Once Upon a Legend

The Elf Chronicles
Diary of a Christmas Elf
Secrets of a Christmas Elf
Adventures of a Christmas Elf

BEN MILLER

DIARY OF A Big Bad Wolf

Illustrated by
ELISA PAGANELLI

SIMON & SCHUSTER

First published in Great Britain in 2024 by Simon & Schuster UK Ltd

Text copyright © Passion Projects Limited 2024
Illustrations copyright © Elisa Paganelli 2024

The right of Ben Miller and Elisa Paganelli to be identified as the author and
illustrator of this work has been asserted by them in accordance with sections 77
and 78 of the Copyright, Designs and Patents Act, 1988.

1 3 5 7 9 10 8 6 4 2

Simon & Schuster UK Ltd
1st Floor, 222 Gray's Inn Road
London WC1X 8HB

Simon & Schuster: Celebrating 100 Years of Publishing in 2024

www.simonandschuster.co.uk
www.simonandschuster.com.au
www.simonandschuster.co.in

Simon & Schuster Australia, Sydney
Simon & Schuster India, New Delhi

A CIP catalogue record for this book is available from the British Library.

HB ISBN 978-1-3985-3036-2
eBook ISBN 978-1-3985-3037-9
eAudio ISBN 978-1-3985-3038-6

Printed and Bound in the UK using
100% Renewable Electricity at CPI Group (UK) Ltd

MIX
Paper | Supporting
responsible forestry
FSC® C171272

For Gran

Wolves'
Clearing

Grandma's
House

Woodsman's
Cottage

Lawrence's
Den

Three Little Pigs

THE Fairytale Woods

Tuesday 21 March

HOWWWWWL!

Winter in the Fairytale Woods is finally over!

Make no mistake, friends, spring has definitely sprung. This very morning, for the first time this

year, I was rudely awoken by the

TWEET-
TWEET-
TWEET of a bird in the

tree above my den.

'The nerve!' I told myself. 'Don't these confounded animals know who they're dealing with? What part of BIG BAD WOLF don't they understand?' Still half asleep, I stomped out of bed, ready to give that chirruping good-for-nothing a piece of my mind, when it struck me:

There's a *bird* in MY TREE!

Now, I'm not a huge fan of birds – the feathers always stick in my throat – and I certainly don't like being woken by them. I mean, these good looks don't come for free! I need my beauty sleep to keep my claws long, my fur thick and my teeth extra sharp and glinty. But seeing this particular

3

bird really cheered me up. Because birds mean spring. And spring means one thing, and one thing only.

FOOD!

Quite frankly, this winter has been tough. Long, hard and hungry. Nothing to eat but crunchy little insects and scrawny, bony rats, not much more than a mouthful of fur and tail. *Yeuch!*

I'm wasting away! But, as my little feathered friend proves, that's all in the past. Any day now, these woods are going to be bursting with tasty newborn snacks . . .

Goodbye, insects! Goodbye, rats!

Hellooooo, little piggies! Hi there, Easter bunnies! Nice to meet you, spring chickens . . .

or should I say . . . nice to EAT you!

Hehehehheh . . .

YUM!

Spring. It's the best!

And this weekend is my favourite event of the

year. Fetch the biggest plate you can find — no,

wait, grab me an even bigger one . . . It's the wolf pack's annual spring barbecue!

There'll be so much delicious meat on that grill, I'm drooling just thinking about it!

HOWWWWWWL!

Wednesday 22 March

Four days to go till the spring barbecue!

Don't you just love a meal you don't have to catch yourself?

And it's just as well I don't have to catch it, because in my current state, I doubt I could run down a three-legged tortoise!

Hunting down a meal is easier for the pack,

of course. Cheating, really, if you
think about it. We lone wolves,
we're at the sharp end. Nothing to
count on but our wits, our charm and
outrageous good looks.

Speaking of which, I have to admit, I'm a tiny bit out of shape. All those long, cold days, with nothing to eat, nothing to do. Just sulking in my den, hiding away from the frost and the rain and the snow . . . I'm all fur and bones! And the fur's not shiny like it should be either. I mean, don't get me wrong, I'm still a fine specimen. My tail and my eyebrows are the bushiest in town, and, if I do say so myself, I practically ooze charm from every pore. It's just . . . I'm a bit underfed. A bit . . . weak. And my pack does not appreciate weakness. I need to raise my game again now spring is here, and get back in shape. Show the pack and the rest of these woods I'm BIG and I'm BAD, and I'm not to be messed with.

9

HOWWWWWL!

So today marks the start of my new spring workout.

I'm thinking something gentle to start with, maybe:

* Fifty star jumps, get the blood pumping
* Fifty press-ups, good for the core
* Fifty pulls-ups, build strong arms

Should be a good start anyway.

Yawn ...

Right, might snatch a quick nap before I jump to it. I'm still in a weakened state, after all. Don't want to do myself an injury.

Nothing a tactical snooze can't fix . . .

Thursday 23 March

Three star jumps
Two press-ups
One pull-up

I am delighted to announce that the spring workout is underway! Admittedly, it was a slow start. I mean, I knew I was a little out of shape, but my goodness! Star jumps are exhausting — all that leaping and arm waving. I was out of breath after the second one, and the third very nearly finished me off. Which didn't leave me with much energy for the other exercises. I mean I just about managed to push

myself up again for the second press-up before collapsing, and I'm not sure the pull-up counts at all . . . I was mainly just hanging there.

Still, I've made a start, which is what really matters, I think?

Maybe ten of each is a more realistic goal to begin with.

I'm sure it will be easier once I get some food inside me.

Speaking of food . . . three sleeps till the barbecue!

HOWwwW W

Friday 24 March

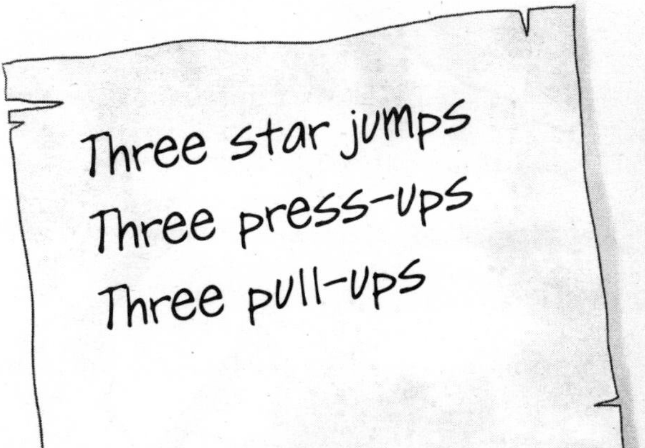

Three star jumps
Three press-ups
Three pull-ups

Managed three of each this morning without collapsing – pretty pleased with that!

Food still a little thin on the ground round here.

I took a swipe at that annoying bird around breakfast time, but he just fluttered off. Munched a leaf covered in caterpillars instead. At least they can't fly away yet!

I'm going to need to get faster if I'm going to make a catch this spring.

Caught sight of the three little pigs over by the Wishing Well while I was out practising my

prowl this morning. *They* obviously haven't had a difficult winter, with their happy skips and their curly tails. Maybe once the barbecue is over and I've got my strength back, I'll treat them to a little game of Predator Versus Prey . . .

Two sleeps to go!

Saturday 25 March

Five star jumps
Five press-ups
Five pull-ups

Halfway to my target! My arms feel more muscly already. Once I've got some protein in me, there'll be no stopping me.

One sleep to go!!!

Sunday 26 March

YAHHHHOOOO!

It's
BARBECUE DAY!!!!!

I was so excited last night, I could hardly sleep, and just when it felt like I had dropped off at last, that little bird started

TWEET-
TWEET-
TWEETING

for the dawn when anyone with eyes could see it was still the middle of the night. Somebody get that bird a watch! As I say, I don't normally go in for eating birds, but I might have to make an exception in his case.

Anyway, I could have done with a teeny bit more beauty sleep, but never mind. I'm off to the river for a quick freshen up, check my reflection, brush my fur, smoooooth down these lovely eyebrows — have to look my best for the pack! — then it's off to get FED.

HOWWWWWL!

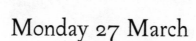

Monday 27 March

Yesterday did not turn out how I expected.

In fact, it was a disaster.

I don't even know where to start. It was bad, bad, BAD from beginning to end.

Well, actually, that's not quite true. There was one silver lining to the day . . . A silver lining in the shape of a little girl in a bright red cape. Little Red, they call her. Not the most original name, I know, but that's the Woods for you. Cat with boots on? Puss in Boots. Young mermaid? The Little Mermaid. Girl with long hair who lives in a tower? High-Haired Helga. I'm kidding, her name's Rapunzel, but you get my drift.

But back to Little Red . . .

I saw her down by the river as I was freshening up for the barbecue and she was strolling over the bridge from the village, heading for the woods. In her red cape, she was pretty obvious – a tasty-looking meal!

Soon as I saw her, I straightened up and twirled my bushy tail round my paw, innocent as you like. Putting on my biggest smile and most charming voice, I said, 'LITTLE RED,

I BELIEVE? I'm Lawrence, your local Big Bad Wolf. Isn't it a fine morning? And what brings you out to the woods today?'

She shot me a withering look as she passed. 'Visiting my grandma, like I do every Sunday,' she said, adding under her breath, 'not that it's any business of yours.'

'Good for you,' I said smoothly, stepping aside so that she could pass. 'See you around, I hope. Found myself a little den back that way.'

'Pack threw you out, did they?' came the less-than-polite reply.

I gave a relaxed laugh. 'I'm a lone wolf,' I said. 'It's a lifestyle choice.'

'Well, Lawrence –' she smirked – 'sometimes choices are just excuses in fur.'

And with that, she flounced off along

29

the path, swinging her basket like she hadn't a care in the world! The cheek! I was about to chase after her, and teach her some manners, when I remembered I was late for the barbecue and, anyway, I didn't want to ruin my appetite, so I let her get away . . . this time!

If only I'd known what was in store, I wouldn't have bothered.

As soon as I stepped into the clearing where the barbecue was being held, I knew something was up. Mum and Dad were nowhere to be seen – off hunting, most likely – and the warm welcome I was hoping for from the rest of the family was sadly lacking. My aunts' and uncles' tails stopped wagging, and my cousins' ears dropped down like they were worried or scared. A few younger wolves whispered to one another, giving me sneaky looks, and an older wolf, who I recognised as one of my father's friends, lowered his gaze and turned away.

It felt just a teensy bit awkward, but I pressed on.

I spotted A-Game over by the grill. A-Game was *always* on the grill, usually cooking some big old juicy hot dogs! Oh my, do I love sausages! I'd been waiting all winter for a treat like this one, and my mouth was slavering as I headed over.

On my way, I bumped into Wolfman, Dad's second-in-command. He was surrounded by his little gang of followers, as usual. If anything, he seemed to have got bigger over winter – how does he manage it? Still, I tried not to show fear. You can't – they can smell it if you do. So I puffed up my chest, casual as could be.

'Wolfman!' I said, slapping him on the back with one hand, and throwing up the other for a high-five. 'Great to see you!'

There was a tense silence. My hand was in the air, a fake smile hanging on my face.

Wolfman looked at my hand, then at me. 'Oh hey, Lawrence,' he said. Then he turned back to his crew and I *definitely* saw him roll his eyes. His crew sniggered quietly. Not one of them said 'hello'.

I let my hand fall – styling it out as best I could with a big fake yawn – then after standing there a minute, nodding to myself and wondering what to do next, I thought, *forget it, their loss*, and walked away.

I won't lie, it stung a little, reminding me why

I left the pack in the first place. But whatever! No one can keep the Big Bad Wolf down.

Besides, I wasn't there to make friends; I was there to eat. A lot. Preferably until I felt a bit sick and slightly disgusted with myself. So I ditched that bunch and headed over to the grill.

'A-Game!' I said, chucking a friendly arm round his shoulder. 'What's cooking?'

A-Game pointed with his barbecue tongs. 'We've got venison, we've got lamb, chicken breast, leg and thigh, oh, and some absolutely scrumptious pork sausages.'

A string of drool slid out of my mouth, and I slurped it back up.

'Here!' I said, holding out both paws. 'Hand it over!'

'Sorry,' replied A-Game, shaking his head. 'Pack members only.' He said it loudly, looking over to make sure Wolfman had heard too. Wolfman and his crew sniggered obligingly.

At this point, I didn't even care about the laughter. I just wanted to know about the meat.

'You're kidding, right? I'll take a sausage, please, A-Game.'

A-Game fixed me with a serious look. 'Listen, Lawrence,' he said. 'We kicked you out for a reason. You never caught anything! You need to fend for yourself.'

'Fend for myself?' I squeaked in surprise. 'I'm starving!'

34

The others chuckled, but it wasn't a kind sound. And A-Game just tutted and shook his head, disapprovingly, then carried on flipping that delicious-looking meat.

'Ha ha, **Lawrence the loser!**' shouted one of Wolfman's crew, and before I knew it, they were all howling and cackling, more like a bunch of stupid hyenas than a pack of wolves.

Well, it didn't feel great. In fact, I almost felt like crying. I'd waited so long for a proper meal, and for company too, if I'm really honest. It was a big disappointment, and I was about to leave with my tail between my legs when I heard a little voice behind me say, 'Hi, Lawrence.'

I turned around. It was Squirt, the runt of the pack. The one wolf who gets it worse than I do!

'Don't mind them,' he whispered. 'They're idiots. How was your winter? You hungry?'

'Depends,' I said, eyeing his plate suspiciously. 'What is that?' The items on his plate didn't look like meat, but I have to admit, they smelled pretty good.

'Well, don't bite my head off,' he said with a shy smile, 'they are veggie, but these pies are really tasty, and I—'

'VEGGIE?' I echoed, pulling a face and pushing the offending item away with my paw. 'Are you out of your mind? Vegetables are disgusting!'

'Want to know a secret?' asked Squirt. He glanced around to make sure no one was listening, then lowered his voice to a whisper. 'I prefer them to meat.'

He offered me his plate one more time. For a split second, a thought flashed in my mind: *At least he didn't have to hurt anything to make those pies.* But then I remembered who I was: the **biggest**, BADDEST wolf in the woods, and my hackles went up.

'Oh why don't you get lost, Squirt!' I barked so loudly, he jumped back in shock and dropped his plate.

I admit, it was harsh, but . . . vegetables! What was he thinking? Besides, I suppose on some level I knew what would happen next. Right on cue, the pack started laughing, but this time at Squirt.

I felt a stab of guilt when I saw the look on his face. His eyes were swimming with hurt as he rummaged around on the ground, picking up his food.

What can I say? It's a dog-eat-dog world – not a dog-eat-hotdog-with-his-pals world, more's the pity. Still, at least I managed to get the attention off me for a second.

And on that note, I decided to quit while the going was good. That's right, I left the wolf pack's annual spring barbecue without having

EATEN
A SINGLE
THING.

My tummy was growling, but my head was held high, my tail bushy and upright, as I strode out of there.

That's that, I thought as I sloped back between the trees. *The pack are dead to me.*

And I really mean it this time. I'm finished with them. I really am. And you know what? That's the way I like it. I don't need friends.

You have to look after yourself in this world. Nobody else is going to put food on your plate. If you want to eat, you have to go out there and chase it down yourself.

So that's precisely what I decided to do. Well, less 'chase' exactly, and more 'wait hungrily on the corner of the bridge, hoping for some poor, unfortunate creature to come skipping past on its way home.'

Yup, top of my list was my silver lining – Little Red. I waited a good hour or so on the corner of that bridge for her to come back from visiting her grandma. But there was no sign of her whatsoever, so I trudged on home, hungry and disappointed.

Today I've just been sulking – I'm so HUNGRY.

Tuesday 28 March

Two star jumps
Two press-ups
Two pull-ups

My workout has taken a hit since the barbecue. Going to have to build up my confidence again.

I'm off to the bridge to see if Little Red walks by. I'm determined to make her my first big meal of spring.

Wednesday 29 March

Five star jumps
Five press-ups
Five pull-ups

Back to pre-barbecue levels!

Managed to swipe some eggs from a bird's nest down by the river. Still no sign of Little Red though.

I'll make sure I'm there same time again on Sunday.

Thursday 30 March

Seven star jumps
Five press-ups
Five pull-ups

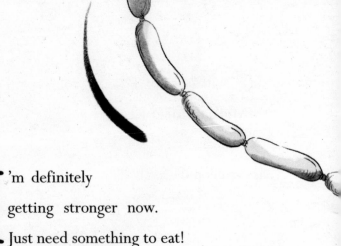

I'm definitely getting stronger now. Just need something to eat!

The problem is, I need food to build muscle, but I need muscle to catch FOOD! What's a wolf to do?

I really could have done with those sausages . . .

Wait!

I've had the most brilliant idea!

I'm going to try and slip over the bridge into the village and steal a string of sausages from the market.

They'll be raw, of course, rather than hot and

sizzling with smoky flavour, but the thought of that full, satisfied feeling . . . It's almost too much to bear!

Maybe I could even hold back a couple – throw a little annual barbecue of my own?

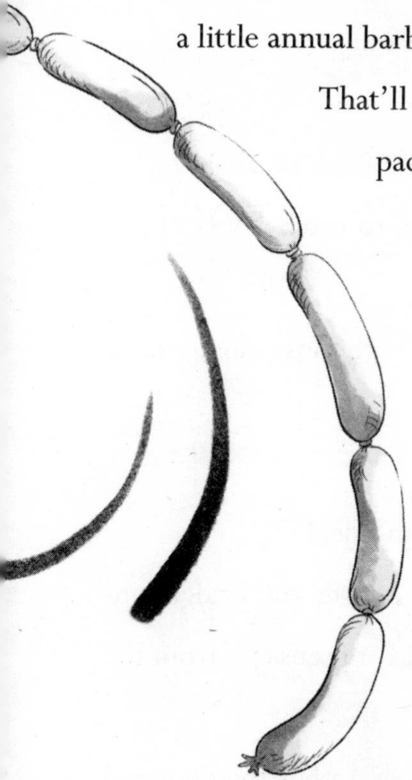

That'll teach that sniggering pack. *Then* they'll see what a success I've made of my life

WITH

NO

HELP

FROM

THEM

WHATSOEVER!

Just have to get past that MOODY
TROLL first . . .

Friday 31 March

Grrr. No sausages.

I was almost halfway across the bridge when that grumpy old troll came lumbering out from his hiding place.

'BRIDGE TAX,' he mumbled, shuffling his full bulk into my path on those little legs of his.

It was the little legs I was counting on . . . I mean, how fast could they really carry him?

'Good day, Mister Troll!' I said, giving him my biggest, most charming smile. 'Bridge tax, of course – let me just . . .' I made a big show of patting my sides. 'Oh blast! I seem to have left the house without my wallet. I don't suppose you'd mind letting me off just this once . . . ?'

'NO TAX, NO CROSSING,' grumbled the troll.

'Completely understandable,' I said, pretending to leave. 'I'll just pop back and get it.'

I knew I would have to play the next bit very carefully indeed . . .

Glancing over my shoulder, I waited till the troll was shuffling back to his station beneath the bridge; then, when his back was turned, I bolted for the other side.

The next thing I knew, there was a sharp pain in my ribs.

'OwWWWW!'

I howled as the troll came bulldozing into me, butting me off the bridge and into the river below with a colossal splash.

I dragged myself up on to the bank, coughing and spluttering, then – with as much dignity as I could muster – parted the pondweed on my head so I could see out.

The troll scowled down at me from the bridge and yelled 'NO TAX, NO CROSSING,' before shuffling off out of sight again.

Well, I wasn't too happy about that, I can tell

you. My fur was caked with river mud, and I'd only just washed it too. Then to top it all off, who should I see strolling over the bridge? Those three ANNOYING little piggies, on their way back from market, no doubt. And what was

worse – they were pointing down at me and

GIGGLING!

They were giggling their little heads off!

I growled at them and they shut up pretty quickly. But not quickly enough.

THEY'LL PAY FOR THAT!

Managed to swipe a fish from the river at least before I headed home, but my fur is not looking its best right now.

Saturday 1 April

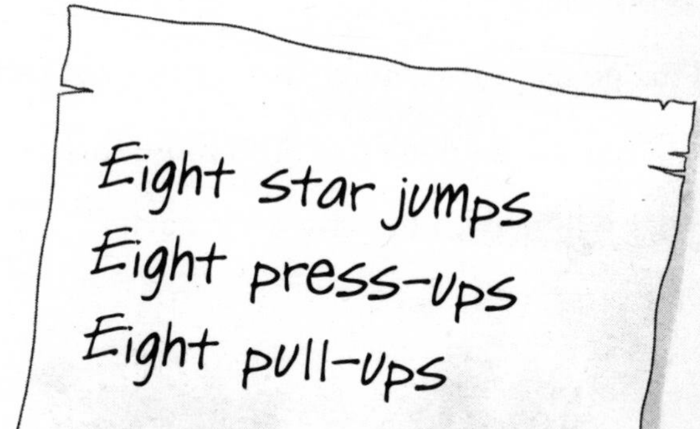

Eight star jumps
Eight press-ups
Eight pull-ups

All right, we're in business now!

Getting stronger and faster every day . . . I've had a couple more fish from the river to keep me going while I build myself back up.

I'm going to devour that little red-caped girl – you see if I don't . . . And those three little piggies will make a lip-smacking starter!

Sunday 2 April

TEN STAR JUMPS!
TEN PRESS-UPS!
TEN PULL-UPS!

I DID IT!!!

I HIT MY TARGET!

I was panting like a dog in a heatwave by the end of it, but still – any way you look at it – I am BACK.

I'm the BIG BAD WOLF, BABY!

I just know Little Red is going to be strolling over that bridge today, and when she does, I'll be waiting, ready to greet her . . . or should I say . . .

EAT HER!!!!

HOWWWWWLLL!!!

Monday 3 April

S till in shock.

Can't actually BELIEVE

what happened yesterday.

I'd better explain . . .

As soon as I'd finished my exercises, I shot down to the river. I wasn't taking any chances.

I'd probably been waiting an hour or two when

at last Little Red came skipping over that bridge. Actually, it was more of a stomp than a skip. I should have taken that as a sign . . .

Anyway, as she crossed the bridge, there I was, leaning nonchalantly up against a tree at the entrance to the woods, looking down at my nails as if I hadn't been waiting hungrily for this moment all winter.

When she passed me, I looked up, feigning surprise and delight. 'Well, HELLO there!' I said. 'Didn't I see you here last week? We have to stop meeting in the woods like this!'

And I laughed my most charming laugh.

This time, she didn't even say anything. She just shot me a withering look and kept on walking. **PHEW** – if looks could kill! Luckily, I'm thick-furred.

'So, you off to Grandma's again?' I said, bounding after her, then slowing to a casual stroll as I entered the woods beside her. 'Woah there, what's the hurry? You should take a minute, stop, look around . . . The woods are beautiful at this time of year. Have you seen all the pretty flowers?'

She glanced across at me. 'Uh-huh,' she said, and kept right on walking.

'Say, what have you got there in that basket anyway? Certainly smells good . . .'

'Pies, for my grandma,' she said. Then she

stopped and, looking me dead in the eye, she said, 'Look, wolf, if you're hungry, why don't you have one?' She held up the basket.

'What's in them?' I asked, bending down to give them a sniff. I have to admit, I was tempted.

'Cheese and vegetables,' she said.

I had a sneaking suspicion I had seen those pies before.

'Where did you get these?' I asked.

'A friend of mine makes them,' she replied.

'You mean . . . Squirt?' I asked.

'That's what you bullying wolves call him,' she replied. 'But he hates that name. I call him Spice Dog.'

I stepped back. 'Thanks, but no thanks . . . I'm on a diet,' I said, patting my stomach.

'Suit yourself,' she said, setting off again.

I can tell you, that girl walks FAST!

I weaved between the trees, keeping pace as best I could, all the while trying to work out my next move.

'So where does Grandma live anyway?' I asked, keeping my voice casual. I was thinking,

If I could somehow

get

to

Grandma's

first . . .

Little Red stopped again. We had come to a sort of crossroads in the woods. There was a path leading straight ahead, and paths off to the left and right. She looked at me a second, as if she was thinking. Then she smiled.

'That way,' she said, pointing off to the right. 'All the way, as far as you can go, about half an hour, 'til the path disappears, and the trees get all old and gnarled and close together. In the shadow of a giant yew tree, you'll see a little house. That's where my grandma lives. You can't miss it.' She smiled again.

I blinked. It took me a moment to respond. I couldn't believe she'd fallen for my cunning plan so easily! I thought I'd have to try a *little* harder than that, but I gathered myself, and went on.

'Here's an idea,' I said, smooth as anything. 'Why not pick Grandma a little posy before you go? Have you seen the flowers down that path?' I pointed straight ahead. 'They are SO BEAUTIFUL . . . Blooms of every colour, and they smell delightful too. I bet Grandma would LOVE a bunch.'

'Good idea,' said Little Red, flashing me a captivating smile. 'I'll be off this way then. Bye.' And with that, she marched straight ahead . . . instead of to the right, where she had literally just told me her grandmother's house was!

She was heading down the wrong path!

This would give me all the time I needed to implement my plan . . .

The first thing would be to trick my way inside . . . by pretending to be Little Red, of course!

By the time the REAL Little Red realised her mistake, and arrived at Grandma's house . . .

Well, I don't need to fill in all the gruesome details, do I? Let's just say, Grandma might be in bed with a terrible headache. In the dark. She'll have a furry face and a *very* wolfish grin . . . and Little Red will have to come right up to the side of the bed to see that . . .

HOWWWWWWL!

Honestly, I had to pinch myself. I couldn't believe my luck. What an idiot she was to fall for such an obvious trick!

I waited till she was out of sight, then raced down the path to the right.

I ran and ran, following the path as it wound deeper into the woods until it disappeared completely. Little Red was right: the trees were different down here — they were older and twistier, and seemed to be huddled closer and closer together. It was dark down this end of the woods too. The tops of the trees were all knotted, so hardly any sunlight could get through.

An owl hooted in a tree above, though surely it was still daytime? It was so dark, it was hard to tell. I slowed my pace a little, hoping I was still going the right way. There was a strange vibe down here — **SPOOKY**, you might say, even for a Big Bad Wolf like me. It didn't seem a nice place for a little old lady to live, but what

do I know about little old ladies, except that they make a wonderful starter? In any case, if I haven't mentioned it yet, let me put you in the picture: I was HUGE HUNGRY.

I was just beginning to worry that maybe I was lost when there it was — a huge twisty old yew tree, and lurking in its shade — a house!

It looked so cute!

I sneaked up to it, inspecting the doors and windows, working out how I was going to get in . . . I had just decided the best way would probably be to go right up and knock on the door, put on a voice and pretend to be Little Red when I noticed this . . . smell. It reminded me of the bakery in the village.

Kind of *biscuity*. And then I realised — it was

gingerbread! The weird thing

was, the smell seemed to be coming from the

house itself. I sniffed again. Yup, no doubt about it. It was coming from the walls. The walls were made of gingerbread!

Well, I'm a wolf, I'm a *carnivore*, my number one dish is meat, but I do have a sweet tooth too. I'm only animal after all! Who *doesn't* like sugar?

Well, it can't hurt to try, I thought. So going up on my hind legs and resting my front paws on the wall, I leaned right in and took a nibble. By my bushy tail, those walls tasted good! Sweet and crisp, with a bit of warm chewiness too. I got lost in that delicious gingerbread, I can tell you. So distracted, in fact, that I didn't notice anyone coming out of the house.

Suddenly a voice from just beside me said, 'Hello.'

I jumped right out of my fur. This was one

scary-looking granny! All warts and wrinkles with a strange, leering gleam in her eyes. A little black cat twisted round and round her ankles as she stood there, smiling at me intently.

'Um, hello!' I said, swallowing my mouthful, and wracking my brains to come up with a new plan. Obviously the old 'pretending to be her granddaughter' trick probably wasn't going to work now she'd seen me. I tried another tack.

'Your, um, granddaughter sent me,' I said. 'Little Red. She said she was sorry, but she wouldn't be able to make it today . . .'

Granny frowned. 'Who?'

'Your granddaughter? Little red cape? Basket of pies?'

She stared at me blankly. *Poor old dear must be losing her marbles*, I thought.

'Just help yourself,' she said, waving at the walls. 'You look like you need to fatten up a bit!' She gave my skin a pinch. 'Let's get some meat on those bones, shall we? Have whatever you like – I particularly recommend the icing on the windowsills. Just watch out for the liquorice beams – we don't want the roof to come crashing down.' Then she laughed and went back inside.

AT LAST, I thought. *Someone who understands me!* So I kept eating and eating, I don't even know for how long . . . A little while later, her head popped round the door again. 'I've got a pot roast in the oven if you'd like some dinner when you're done?'

WOW – sugar for main course – meat for pudding! Here was a woman after my own heart – even if she was SCARY! She didn't have to ask me twice . . . I whizzed right in there, tongue hanging out and drooling. She was holding the door of the oven open and smiling.

'Go on, take a look inside . . .' she said. I slowed my pace, hovering by the kitchen door. For some reason, I was starting to feel a bit uneasy. 'Go on, take a look . . . just lean in . . .' she said, smiling hungrily.

WAIT A MINUTE!

I know how this story ends! I thought. *This woman isn't a grandma . . . She's a witch! She doesn't want to feed me. It's* ME *that's on the menu!* I'M *what's going to be cooking in that oven if I don't get out of here* SHARPISH . . .

'Hey!' she cried, as I bolted out of the

front door and raced off into the woods.

'Come back!'

But I didn't listen – I ran, and I ran, and I didn't stop running till I was safely back in my den. And I've been too scared to leave it all day.

Tuesday 4 April

S till too cross to do my exercises this morning.

It's slowly dawning on me . . .

Little Red lied to me! She TRICKED me!

She knew exactly where she was sending me and nearly got me EATEN!

Who does she think she IS?

NOBODY eats the BIG BAD WOLF! I'm the one that does the eating round here!

Speaking of which, I really DO need to get a few calories on board. I seem to be getting weaker rather than stronger. And I'm going to need all my strength for my revenge.

I'm off out right now to catch myself some

FOOD.

I'm back! Exhausted.

I nearly killed myself chasing a rabbit! Those things are FAST. I was gaining on it, when I tripped on a big old tree root and went flying.

On the upside, next to where I landed I noticed

a squirrel on the ground. I prodded it, but it wasn't moving. Must have fallen from the tree.

Well, I didn't bury it and give it a funeral, put it that way.

I gobbled it down in one. No sense letting good meat go to waste. I'm pretty sure it's what the squirrel would have wanted.

Feeling a bit better after some protein. Think I'll try my luck with the troll again tomorrow.

There are some fresh sausages in that village, which most definitely have my name on . . .

Wednesday 5 April

Grrrrn, that blasted troll! There I was, right in the middle of the bridge, when out he shuffles directly into my path.

'BRIDGE TAX,' he muttered. The way he says it, I'm not convinced he gets much job satisfaction.

'Well, I'm glad you asked,' I purred, fluffing

up my eyebrows to pick out the amber in my eyes. 'I've actually brought you a lovely . . . Wait, is that a GOAT?' I said, pointing. The second his little trollish back was turned, I bolted for the other end of the bridge.

'Owwwwww!'
SPLASH.

'NO TAX, NO CROSSING.'

For a troll, he really is fast.

As I stood there, looking like a drowned rat, I heard a little noise coming from behind me.

'Hehe, hehe, hehe,' it croaked.

There was a frog sat on the riverbank – and it was LAUGHING at me!

Pretending I hadn't seen it, I swam downstream, hauled myself out, then sneaked back towards it. Then, when was I close enough, I pounced!

'HA!' I said, closing my paws around it, but it was so slippery, it shot right through them. The mud it was sitting on turned out to be rather slippery too, and I skidded off the bank and back into the river.

'Hehe, hehe, hehe,' it laughed as it hopped away to safety.

Grrrrrrrr.

Thursday 6 April

Half a star jump
Zero press-ups
Zero pull-ups

Rained all day.

Stayed in the den.

Ate a woodlouse.

Spat it out again.

Then half an hour later, I felt so hungry, I ate it again.

How has my life come to this?

Friday 7 April

More rain.

Palmed a handful of worms that had wriggled their way to the surface. Then felt a bit sick and went back to bed.

Saturday 8 April

J ust drizzling now, but still, it doesn't make you want to go outside.

Since the rain, I noticed these little . . . things, cropping up around my den.

Little umbrella-looking things – white on top, brown underneath. What are they called? Mushy something-or-other?

Was so hungry, I decided to try a little nibble.

YUK.

No thanks.

Think I'll save my appetite for the main course . . .

It's Sunday tomorrow, and if it's the last thing I do, I'm going to catch that little red-coated girl!

Sunday 9 April

ALL RIGHT!
LET'S DO
THIS!

I'm running on empty, so I'm going to keep this plan short and swift.

1. Jump out
2. Gobble girl whole
3. Job done

No need to overcomplicate.

DON'T
EVEN
ASK.

Tuesday 11 April

Well this time she's really done it. I was cross before, but now **I'M FURIOUS.** I'm spitting fire and vengeance with every breath. This girl is HISTORY. Mincemeat!

You can trick the Big Bad Wolf once, but *twice?* No way.

Well, I mean, yes, I guess she *did* trick me twice. But she won't manage it a third time, that's for sure. She won't be ALIVE to trick me a third time.

I spent all yesterday too fuming to write. But I suppose I'd better explain what happened, though it's not a story I'll enjoy recounting.

So I went to the bridge on Sunday, bright and early, but *this* time I hid behind the tree so I could see her before she saw me, in case she decided to run.

To my delight, when she walked by, I saw she was with those three giggly little piggies!

It seemed too good to be true . . . This revenge was going to be sweet!

Fresh Little Red with a side of pork!

I waited till they'd passed the tree I was hiding behind; then, rather than showing myself, I followed, all secretive, jumping from tree to tree, flattening myself against the trunks so there was no chance of them spotting me.

Just before they got to the crossroads, I whizzed on ahead, slipping silently past them through the trees. Then I leaped out.

'HA!' I shouted.

I was right in their path now.

The three little piggies squealed and clutched each other. Little Red whispered something to them; then they hurried off down the path to the left.

'HEY!' I shouted. 'Where do you think you're going?'

I was about to run after them when she said, 'Wait . . .'

'What?' I said, spinning round angrily.

'I just wanted to say . . . sorry.'

'SORRY?' I narrowed my eyes. 'You sent me to the WITCH!

I nearly got EATEN.'

She frowned at me, cocking her head on one side. 'Eaten? You mean, like you wanted to eat me and my grandma?' she said, blinking up at me all innocent.

'Well, um, no . . . I mean, MAYBE . . . but . . .'

I wasn't quite sure what to say to that. How did she know that had been my plan all along? I suppose she had a point, but that's how it goes, right? I didn't ask to be top of the food chain . . .

'Anyway,' she went on, 'it was a mean trick, and I'm sorry. I want to make it up to you. Are you hungry?'

'Errrrr, YES! I mean . . . *why*?' I added, more cautiously. I knew it had to be a trap, but appetite got the better of me. I was hungry! I was

STARVING! I couldn't deny it.

'Well,' she said, leaning in and whispering, 'how would you like to eat three delicious little piggies?'

I raised an eyebrow. 'You mean, your *friends?* The ones you were with just now?'

'Uh-huh,' she said, like it was no big deal.

Well, I had to admire that kind of coldness. That moral flexibility will get you a long way in these woods, make no mistake. She really had it together, with her neat cape and her sweet little basket. If I hadn't wanted her for my dinner, I would probably have asked her if she wanted to be friends.

'I'm interested,' I said. 'Keep talking.'

'Come,' she said, beckoning me down the path to the left. 'I'll show you where their house is. They're hiding in there now. I told them I'd lead you in the wrong direction, but . . .' She turned and shrugged, then carried on down the path.

I followed after Little Red. I was getting excited about this idea, my tongue was out and my mouth was beginning to water, when it hit me again. This HAD to be a trick, didn't it?

'Wait a minute, wait a minute,' I said, stopping. 'Okay, I get it. So this is the bit where you lead me to some house in the woods then tell me, "Go on! Go right in! This is the three little piggies' house!" and actually it's the three BEARS' house . . . Is that it? Forget it, shortcake! Do you think I was born yesterday?'

'No way, I'm SERIOUS,' she said, taking my paw and leading me on. 'Listen, those piggies, they're annoying, always hanging around, always

GIGGLING.'

'Pff,' I said, 'you're telling me!'

'Right?' She rolled her eyes at me. 'Trust me, you'd be doing me a favour! But if I show you where they live, you have to promise me one thing.'

'And what might that be?' I asked suspiciously.

'Not to eat me,' she said, batting her eyelashes. Her eyes were rich brown, like ripe horse chestnuts. 'It's hard being a fairy-tale girl,' she sighed, swinging my paw as we walked. 'There are evil witches and scary wolves and giant ogres everywhere just ready to pounce. All I want to do is visit my grandma in peace. So if I help you, do you promise?'

She stopped and looked at me.

'Sure,' I said, casually crossing my fingers behind my back.

We strolled on through the woods together. I kept stealing little glances at her. I had to hand it to her . . . this girl was no chicken. Walking deep into the woods with the Big Bad Wolf? She had some nerve!

But she was stupid too. Did she really think I wasn't going to eat her right afterwards? I'd swallow each one of those piggies whole – one, two, three – no more than a snack for a Big Bad Wolf like me: a mere palate cleanser, a small plate, a little *antipasti* before moving on to my main course, the *entrée*, the *pièce de résistance*, the . . .

I noticed Little Red was looking at me. 'What?' I said, wiping the drool from my mouth.

'I said where's your den?'

Oh right, I thought to myself, *are we making conversation now? Okay . . . get to know your dinner before you eat it. Sure, why not?*

'In quite a nice area, actually,' I replied. 'Brushwood Hollow? Back over the bridge – or around it if you can't pay the tax – take the left fork – not the right, that goes to the village – follow that for about five minutes, there's a thicket there . . .'

'I know it,' she said. 'There are loads of mushrooms, right? I sometimes go there to gather them.'

'*Mushrooms* . . .' I repeated. 'That's what they're called! Those little white umbrella things?'

She laughed. 'The very same. Tasty, those ones, too!'

I made a face.

'Not for you, eh? They're better cooked. You should try them fried in butter . . .

DELICIOUS!'

'I'm more of a pork chops kind of guy, know what I mean?' I said. 'All meat, hold the veg.'

'I noticed,' she said, grinning.

'So what about Grandma?' I asked, trying to sound casual.

'What about her?'

'Where *does* she live?'

Little Red gave me one of her looks. 'Like I'd tell you!'

111

Well, I had to laugh at that. I guess she's not **completely** stupid.

'Here we are,' she said, stopping in front of a tiny little house. 'Put your ear to the door – you'll hear them . . .'

I sneaked up to the house, and did as she said. The wall was scratchy, like it was made of straw or something. After a moment, I heard giggles coming from inside. She was right! I'd know that piggy giggling anywhere!

'So, how do I get in?'

'Well,' she said, looking it up and down, 'It's only made of straw – and it doesn't look very well built to me. A big, strong wolf like you could probably just **HUFF** and **PUFF** and blow it down, right?'

'Right,' I said. I wasn't convinced, but maybe

I didn't know my own strength? If Little Red thought I could, then I at least had to try. I didn't want to lose face.

So I took a few practice deep breaths, in and out, in and out, to warm up. *Good job I've been working out*, I thought.

Then when I was ready, I took an extra-deep breath in and, squeezing my eyes tight shut, I pursed my mouth up and blew out as hard as I could.

I opened an eye. The house was still there.

I did the same again – all the way in . . . and out again, hard as I could.

Twice more.

By now, I was beginning to feel really dizzy.

I looked over at Little Red. She seemed to be having a coughing fit.

'Try again,' she said. 'I think I saw the walls move a little last time!'

'Really?' I asked hopefully.

'A little bit . . .'

Filled with renewed hope, I tried again. And again. And again.

Soon, I had collapsed on the floor, head spinning and exhausted. I was so hungry, and so tired.

Little Red came over and sat down on the ground next to me. 'Not working, eh?' she asked, the corners of her mouth twitching.

I hung my head. 'I'll try again in a minute. Just need to get my strength back.'

'Look,' she said, 'just a suggestion, but are you SURE you wouldn't just like one of these pies? They're so delicious. It'd be a whole lot easier . . .'

At the word 'pies', my eyes lit up; then they narrowed.

'They're vegetarian! Why would I want them when I've got three little piggies right here?'

'Okay, okay! Keep your fur on – it was just an idea,' she said with a sigh. 'Look, there's a chimney on the roof. See it? Maybe you could drop down through it and surprise them?'

She was right! It was a big one too . . .

I didn't have to be told twice. I was up those straw walls and on to that roof in a heartbeat; then, without a second thought, I squeezed myself into the chimney and dropped right down, bum first, into the fireplace.

'GOTCHA!' I shouted.

I looked around the room . . . It was empty.
Not a piggie in sight . . . just . . . smoke. Coming
from the fire. Which I was sat in!

OW
OWW
OWWW
OWWW
HOWWWW

LLLL!!!

I howled and leaped out of the fireplace . . . My bottom was scorched and the end of my beautiful bushy tail was on fire!

I ran out of the door, looking for something to put it out with . . . and what should I see?

Those three giggly little piggies, sat there with Little Red – all four of them, pointing and laughing!

They weren't alone either. A crowd seemed to have gathered – there was a goat and a hen and,

117

randomly, some boy with a cow, and even a bunch of dwarves – a whole crowd of the Fairytale Woods' finest – all after a front-row seat to the joke of the century . . . Me.

'You're all going to PAY FOR THIS!' I shouted. 'I'm going to EAT YOU ALL!'

And with that, I ran to the river as fast as I could to put out my burnt tail.

Their laughter was still ringing in my ears as I jumped into the murky water.

Or I thought it was.

Then I looked up and saw it was the troll. He was having a good laugh too.

Wednesday 12 April

Don't feel like writing today.

Thursday 13 April

Whatever I do, everyone ends up laughing at me.

The pack laugh at me.

Even that grumpy old troll was laughing at me . . . and that's got to be the first time I've even seen him SMILE.

Little Red laughs at me, and I was starting

to think she actually cared. What's *wrong* with me? I've lost my killer instinct, thinking a stupid little girl in a red cape might want to be friends. Wolves and girls should never work together – it's just not natural. And as for those stupid little piggies . . .

Yup, guess I'm just a BIG joke.

REALLLLLLY funny.

HA HA HA HA.

Saturday 15 April

I've decided. Enough's enough. The joke's over.

I've had it with being laughed at.

I've had it with being tricked.

I'll show them!

No more charming smiles. No more jokes.

NO MORE MISTER NICE WOLF.

Everyone round here seems to have forgotten who they're dealing with! I'm a SHARK! I'm a KILLER! I'm top of the food chain! NOBODY messes with the Big Bad Wolf and gets away with it!

HOWWWWWWL!

Sunday 16 April

All right, so here's the plan. And if I say so myself, which I do, it's a beauty.

I'm going to wait up a tree in the woods by the crossroads, and when that scheming Little Red walks by, I'm just going to

POUNCE.

I'm not going to give her a chance to trick me, or distract me with one of her disgusting cheese pies.

I'm going to jump right on top of her and gobble her up, before she gets a chance to say ANYTHING.

Before she can even open her mouth, I'll open mine – and swallow her whole!

Monday 17th April

At the bottom of a well.

Not quite ready to journal this.

Need to process things first.

Still down the well. The sun is going down now.

Will be too dark to write soon, so I guess I'd better get this story over with. So glad I brought my diary with me — it's something to keep me busy while I'm stuck here.

Anyway . . . there I was, waiting up that tree, as planned. I saw Little Red coming from a way away.

Unfortunately, she saw me too. HOW, I still don't know.

'That you up there, Wolfy?' she asked, slowing her pace. 'Listen, before you say anything, I know you're angry, and you should be. It was a mean trick I played on you . . . and I actually felt bad afterwards. How's your tail?'

I stayed in my hiding place. From where Little Red was standing, it must have looked like the leaves were talking.

'I believe you,' I said, making it clear I one hundred per cent didn't. 'You looked like you felt bad as you were LAUGHING YOUR HEAD OFF.'

'Well, it was a *little* funny too, you have to admit . . .'

'Oh SURE, it was HILARIOUS. Let's all have a good laugh at Wolfy. Well, you've had your fun . . . now it's time for MINE!'

I growled and jumped down from the tree. Little Red jumped backwards just in time.

'Honestly, wolfy,' she said, backing away as I stalked towards her, 'I *did* feel bad . . . but what are we supposed to do? Just let you EAT us? You can't just go around munching whoever you like. We've all got a right to live in the Fairytale Woods.'

Little Red was backed against a tree now. Nowhere left to run. I smiled and licked my lips.

'I mean, can't we all just get along?' she finished, starting to look a bit worried.

'Get along?' I said, pushing my face into hers. 'You want us to GET ALONG?'

I was warming to my topic now. I was hotting up. In fact, my blood was boiling.

'Oh yeah, let's all just GET ALONG . . .' I scoffed, pacing back and forth in front of her, waving my arms around like a windmill. 'Let's all be BEST FRIENDS FOR EVER and go skipping through the woods together, arm in arm . . . says the girl who tried to get me EATEN and then almost had me BURNED ALIVE!'

I finished with a flourish, turning back to her, hands on hips.

Huh? Where'd she go?

To my horror, I glimpsed a flash of red, disappearing down the path to the left.

HOW wwww WLLLL!!!

She had tricked me AGAIN!

I roared after her, weaving through the trees, zipping in and out, leaping over fallen branches and rocks. I was tiring quickly, though. Panting and out of breath, I just wasn't fit enough for the chase, plus I had a terrible stitch in my side. I was slowing down, ready to throw the towel in, when I noticed the flash of red seemed to be getting bigger, and closer, until . . .

Wait, had she STOPPED?

I slowed my pace, smiling as I stalked up to her, low and slow.

She was puffing and panting and holding her sides. 'I can't go on . . .' she said, shaking her head. 'You're too fast. You're just going to have to eat me. I give up.'

'Ha!' I shouted triumphantly. 'Not laughing now, are you! Thought you could make a fool of the Big Bad Wolf? Well, you'll be sorry you ever laughed at me!'

I stood there a minute.

Little Red was looking at me, head on one side.

It was time to get this over with, get my revenge. I knew that. But I hesitated. I wasn't quite sure why.

Then I remembered the sound of laughter —
Little Red, those piggies, the troll, the frog, the
pack, *all of them*, giggling and sniggering and
smirking — and, feeling a surge of fury, I leaped
up high into the air, claws out, ready to . . .

Looking down, I saw that she'd stepped out of
the way and beneath her was . . .

Oh no, I thought . . . as d
o
w
n

I fell, d
o
w
n and d
o
w
n,

135

right down to the bottom of an old empty well.

I hit the ground with a thud —

— and looked up.

Far above me was a circle of daylight. Little Red's face appeared in it, eclipsing the light.

'Honestly, wolfy, you can believe me or not, but I AM sorry . . . I just don't want to get eaten!'

'Go away,' I shouted, turning away from her, towards the wall.

'Come on, why don't we call a truce?' she said. 'Want me to throw a rope down for you?'

'JUST
LEAVE ME
ALONE,'

I screamed.

'Fine,' she sighed. 'Suit yourself.' And with that, she was gone.

Dark now. Too tired to figure out how to escape.

Just going to curl up here and sleep and try again in the morning.

Tuesday 18 April

S till here. Can't crawl out.

Walls
too
steep.

Broke half my nails trying.

Little Red will pay for this!

Not sure if it's day or night. I must be hallucinating. I thought I saw my father standing next to me, lit up as if he was a wolf-shaped lantern with a candle inside.

'Lawrence,' he said in that booming voice of his. 'What's happening here? Why are you stuck down a well?'

'What – this well?' I asked. 'Just fancied a change of scene. Bit of me time!'

'That little girl tricked you again, didn't she?' he sneered, prodding my chest with a long, sharp claw. 'Tricked by a little girl. You're soft. You always were.'

'Not soft!' I protested. 'Sensitive!'

But he had that look in his eye he always

seemed to save just for me. Disappointment.

'Your first hunt with the pack, we had that baby fawn surrounded. "Take him, Lawrence!" I said. "Pounce!" And you –' he prodded me in the chest again with that claw of his – 'you let him go.'

'He slipped through my paws!' I protested.

'You'll never be one of us,' my dad growled, baring his long, sharp teeth. 'You just don't have that killer instinct.'

Then he vanished in a puff of smoke.

I won't be able to last down here much longer . . .

Wednesday 19 April?

Lost track of time.

All I know is, it's dark.

Thought I saw a face appear in the circle of sky above, but it was just the moon, full and round and . . .

HOWWWW WLLLL!!!

Thursday 20 April

AT LAST!!!
I AM
FREE!!!

Luckily, an old woodcutter heard my howl, and threw a rope down for me, but I was too weak to climb up it. He disappeared and I howled and HOWLED, thinking he'd left me, but then he reappeared a minute later and threw the rope down again, this time with a bucket tied to the end. Red-faced with shame, I climbed into the bucket and let myself be pulled to safety. I got over my humiliation pretty quickly, though, when I saw what that old woodcutter had waiting for me at the top – a great big bowl of stew!

I can tell you – and I'm not ashamed to admit it – tears welled in my eyes. Such kindness! I mean, he was probably just feeding me so that I didn't eat him, but still. I descended gratefully on that bowl like it was my last supper . . . It had been a long time since I'd had a good, hearty meal like that, and BOY did it taste incredible. I didn't even realise until halfway through that it was entirely made of vegetables. I didn't even hesitate, just WOLFED it down all the same.

And that's not even the half of it – it gets better! I hadn't been wasting my time down that well – I'd come up with a plan. There was just one piece of the puzzle missing, and as I drained the bowl dry, I realised this dopey old woodcutter might just be that missing piece . . .

I'll tell you everything tomorrow. Right now, my eyes are closing. It's my first night in my own den with a belly full of food for as long as I can remember and I'm going to snore like Sleeping Beauty!

Friday 21 April

Phew! Just tried to do a few press-ups. No luck. Managed to push myself up once; then I collapsed and couldn't get up again, just lay there on the ground, panting. Guess I'm really out of shape now.

The meal last night was good and much needed,

but after weeks of next to no eating, followed by four nights sleeping down a well with only the grubs for dinner and company, I wasn't feeling exactly *refreshed*.

Besides, I have to conserve what little strength I have, because *this* weekend is going to be the one.

I know where Grandma's house is!

Yup, that's right. As I was finishing my stew last night, the old woodcutter said, 'So, what's a wolf like you doing all the way out here anyway? Don't normally see your type at this end of the woods.'

I straightened, coughed politely, and, wiping the stew from my chin, I said, 'Actually, I wonder if you might be able to help me. I was looking for a little old lady's house – maybe you know her?

She's got a granddaughter, Little Red, cute little thing, wears a red cape?'

The woodcutter's face turned serious. 'Now, what does a wolf like you want with good people like them? You've had your stew. You go on home now and leave them alone.'

'My dear sir,' I said, pulling a wounded face, 'you've got me all wrong! Little Red is my friend. Sadly she's not very well. She ate a mouldy sausage at a party, and can't make it to her grandmother's this Sunday like she normally does. So she asked if I might deliver some baked goods for her. Only I got lost and fell down that well, and in the end I was down there so long, I had to eat them to stay alive . . .'

The woodcutter looked puzzled. 'I even ate the basket,' I added hastily. He smiled uncertainly.

'I need to put this right. Check that Red is on the mend, then pay a visit to her grandma. You don't happen to know where her house is, do you?

There was a long pause, and for a second I thought I'd gone too far. There's no *way* the woodcutter would believe a story like that from a wolf like me.

But he suddenly took off his hat and bowed his head. 'My apologies, Mister Wolf. Clearly, I've misjudged you. If there's one thing I've learned in my long life, it's that you can never judge a book by its cover – or in this case, a wolf by its teeth. I forgot that. I'm sorry.'

Ha!

That's right!

The old softy fell for it, hook, line and sinker!

'How true indeed,' I said, doing my best not to

smirk. 'I see with age comes wisdom.'

'Along with a stiff back and achy knees – but you can't have everything!'

He laughed loudly at his own joke, and I chuckled along obligingly. Then I waited for the old man to give up the goods. I coughed. He was still chuckling. It seemed his memory was in as bad a shape as his knees.

'Um, so . . .' I prompted. 'Grandma's house?'

'Ahh, yes! Right . . . well, you were close! We're practically neighbours. See those three big oak trees over there? There's a clearing between them, and that's where you'll find her. So as long as you can make your way back here, you should be fine . . . Think you can do that?'

'Oh definitely,' I said, although in truth I wasn't sure at all. Where was I? I had just been chasing that flash of red . . . I hadn't been paying attention to where I was going.

'If you could just point me in the direction of the crossroads,' I gushed, 'I'm sure I can work it out . . . Oh, and if it's not too much trouble, perhaps a hunk of bread for the journey home?'

I'd had another one of my ideas, you see . . .

All the way home, I'll drop a trail of crumbs so I can find my way back.

And I'm going to memorise the route so when Sunday comes, I'll know exactly where to go. I'm not leaving anything to chance now!

It's later now and I've just got in. I really do not like birds.

Not ONE LITTLE BIT.

Grrr. Stupid idiots ate all the crumbs!

Perhaps I should have seen that coming . . .

Been walking ALL DAY. Couldn't find the trail anywhere. Came home exhausted and hungry.

Will try again tomorrow.

Saturday 22 April

At last . . . I am at Grandma's house! Too tired to be excited, though, and it's too late to head home. Got spots in front of my eyes. Possibly starving? Tried to snatch a squirrel from a low branch for dinner, but it hopped away from me easily and I lost my balance and fell over.

Just going to sleep here, where I fell, under this tree, and rest. Till tomorrow . . .

Sunday 23 April

And so here we are at last – the day of reckoning!

Little Red has tricked me, lied to me . . . LAUGHED at me.

I've been almost eaten by a witch, and nearly burned alive . . .

I've barely eaten or slept this week – this

whole spring, in fact.

I've spent four nights down a well, two lost in the woods, and now finally – FINALLY – it's payback time!!

HOWWWWWLLLL!!!

Oof, shouldn't howl. That made me feel dizzy. I need to conserve what energy I have left.

Still, I'm here now. I am literally camped outside Grandma's house. Nothing and no one can stop me now!

Still an hour or so till Little Red arrives. Plenty of time to get in there and gobble up

Grandma. I doubt a little old lady will put up much fight. Then all I have to do is lie in wait, digesting my starter, and wait for my main course to come knocking.

Let's face it, Red's got NO IDEA what she's up against. She's practically going to walk right into my mouth! It'll be like taking candy from a baby. EASY.

Okay . . . This is it. Here we go.

I'm going in!

Something the somethingth
of something

No idea what day it is.

Woah, what time is it? Is it dark already?

Wait – what DAY is it? How long have I been asleep?

WHERE AM I?

Oh no, oh no, oh no . . .

I'm not still . . . ??

Oh no, I am.

I'M IN
GRANDMA'S
BED!!

But where's Grandma? And where is Little Red?

This is not good. I am NOT enjoying the memories that are coming back.

And –

'Ow WWWW!'

my tummy hurts so much. And obviously not for the good reason that I ate a hearty grandma-and-granddaughter two-course meal.

Nope, I have the distinct memory that I didn't. That I ate . . .

Oh no . . .

I can't believe this has happened to me.

Why am I still here . . . ?

And, wait – is that . . . ? Is there someone else in the room . . . ? Over there, in the rocking chair, asleep?

Is that . . . ?

That can't be . . .

Is it . . . ?

All I can see is a vague red blur. Can't keep my eyes open. Must sleep.

Tuesday 25 April

I'm awake again. It's daytime now, and there's nobody in the rocking chair. Maybe I dreamed it all.

I've just tried to get up, hoping to sneak back to my den, but I was too weak, and my tummy is still *really* sore.

Everything's a horrible blur. I don't really want

to remember . . . but I guess I should.

I remember . . . knocking on Grandma's door . . .

'That you, Red?' called a voice from inside. 'It's open, dear. Come in.'

Well, she didn't have to ask me twice. I kicked the door open dramatically.

'Grandma!' I bellowed. 'We meet at last!'

Grandma peered at me over her glasses. 'Who are you, dear? Do I know you?'

'You might know *of* me . . . I have a certain fame round these parts,' I said, marching into the centre of the room, and standing there, hands on hips, waiting for her to recognise me and SCREAM in terror.

Grandma was still peering over her glasses. 'No, I don't think so, dear. Can I help you?'

'Can you help me?' Well, that got my scruff up, I can tell you! 'I am the BIG BAD WOLF!' I bristled. 'I don't need *your* help.'

'Okay, dear,' said Grandma, getting out of bed. 'Are you sure? Only . . . your fur looks awfully dusty and you seem a little unsteady on your feet. Are you unwell?'

Then, to my surprise, Grandma started walking towards me with a concerned look on her face – and do you know what that woman did? She put a hand on my forehead!

'You seem a little hot, dear . . . Can I get you a glass of water?'

Furiously, I batted the hand away. 'I do not want a glass of water . . . I am here to FEED!'

'Okay, dear. Well my granddaughter will be here with some pies soon. Why don't you settle yourself down in that rocking chair, and—'

'SETTLE DOWN????'

I shouted. 'I will NOT settle down, and I don't want any stupid pies. I am going to eat YOU!!!!'

And with that, I pounced. Or I thought I was pouncing, but a moment later, I found myself on the floor. I seemed to have lost my balance and fallen over. My head was spinning. I was seeing two of everything.

Next thing I knew, Grandma had picked up her broom and was trying to sweep me out of the door, like I was a stray dog off the street!

'Go on, shoo!' she said. 'If you're going to be like that, just get out . . .'

'STOP THAT!' I shouted, shielding my head. I managed to wrestle the broom away from her and chuck it across the room, but the effort left me dizzy and confused. Finding myself unable to stand, I gave a half-hearted lunge, somehow ending up with my jaws wrapped around her shoe. For a while, she dragged me along the floor towards the door. When I refused to let go, she wiggled and wiggled and wiggled her leg, which made my head spin even more, until her foot came loose, leaving her shoe clutched in my mouth. Grandma grabbed her coat and ran for the door.

'ARRRGGGHHH!!'

I bellowed in frustration, and in the next breath, I sucked up the shoe by mistake . . . and swallowed it!

Grandma turned to shake her head at me sadly, then walked out.

Okay, okay, okay . . . I thought. *It's not the end of the world.* So Grandma got away. She was never the main course anyway. I mean, neither was A SHOE, but never mind!

I had to think straight. But it was hard . . . My tummy did not feel right and neither did my head.

Eventually, I managed to pull myself up from the floor. Stumbling over to the wardrobe, I selected a rather fetching pink dressing gown and a large fluffy shawl, and, wrapping myself up in them, climbed gratefully into bed.

The sheets were so cool and calming and there was a cosy patchwork quilt to snuggle under. Once I was in there, I spotted a very comfy-looking white lace bonnet hanging on the bedpost.

The perfect disguise!

I was exhausted, and my tummy was starting to ache. I must have closed my eyes for a moment, because the next thing I knew, I heard a voice from the door saying, 'Grandma?'

Quickly, I pulled the duvet up to my chin, arranged the bonnet, and waited. My heart was thumping loudly. This was it! This was the moment I had waited for!

'Why, Grandma,' said Little Red, 'why's the door open? Is everything okay?'

I moaned in response. I didn't exactly mean to, but the shoe was wedged in my stomach,

and I was in a lot of pain.

'Why, Grandma,' said Little Red again, stepping towards the bed, 'what's wrong with your voice? Are you sick?'

'Maybe just a little, dear child,' I said feebly. No acting required, considering the state I was in. 'Come closer, so I can see you more clearly.'

She sat on the edge of the bed, right next to me. That pesky girl was so close, I could just reach out and grab her! I took a deep breath, preparing myself . . .

'Why, Grandma!' she exclaimed. 'What big arms you have!'

Eek! My fur stood on end. Was she on to me? I needed to think quickly . . .

'All the better to hug you with,' I said.

It was a bit of a lame line, admittedly, but it was the best I could do at the time.

'And what big ears you have!' said Little Red.

I frowned, suspiciously. If she could see my ears, she one hundred per cent knew I was a wolf, surely?

But her face was unreadable.

'All the better to hear you with,' I warbled.

'And what big eyes you have!'

'All the better to see you with,' I said uncertainly. I'd started down this track and there was no turning back now.

'And what big teeth you've got!'

Was that a smile curling on her lips? I couldn't be sure, so I stayed in character.

'All the better to . . .'

I paused for dramatic effect. This was truly a moment to savour. I was finally going to get my own back on this smug little girl, enjoy a square meal, and win back the pack, all in one joyous gulp . . .

'EAT YOU WITH!'

I roared.

Mustering every last ounce of energy I had, I lunged forward.

Like a ninja, Little Red . . . well, she stood up. And I rolled off the bed on to the floor.

'OWWW

OWWW

OwWW

MY

TUMMMMY

OwWWW!!!!'

I yelped. I had landed right on it and it was REALLY sore now. I clutched my stomach. I could feel the shape of the shoe inside me, solid as a brick.

As I lay there, yelping and howling, Grandma came rushing back in with that old woodcutter.

'Oh, thank goodness you're all right!' said Grandma to Little Red. 'We heard the cries from outside . . . I thought maybe . . .'

'I'm fine,' said Little Red cheerfully. 'But our friend here doesn't seem to be doing so well.'

'Is that my bonnet?' asked Grandma, puzzled.

'I *know* this wolf!' said the woodcutter. 'He asked for directions here.'

'And you GAVE them to him?' said Little Red. 'What were you thinking?'

'Sorry,' replied the woodcutter. 'He seemed so friendly.'

'Why is he rolling around like that?'

I could hear their voices above me, but my eyes were closing now, the pain was so great.

'He ate my shoe,' said Grandma.

'He *what?*' said Little Red.

'He seemed very disturbed.'

'No kidding,' replied Little Red. 'I think he's delirious. I mean, why else would he dress up as you and climb into your bed?'

I heard Little Red sigh. A moment later, she crouched down beside me.

'Poor wolfy,' she said. 'He must be so hungry. I tried to help him, but he just won't eat vegetables.'

I felt a hand on my head. It was soft and warm. Tears sprang to my eyes.

'It's okay,' she whispered. 'You'll be okay . . .'

And then I guess I passed out, because that's the last thing I remember.

Wait, I think I hear footsteps outside . . . but I'm so tired. I'm just going to close my eyes again.

Thursday 27 April

Well, I tell you, these woods are full of surprises!

I woke up so confused, still in Grandma's house and feeling awful, though the shoe-shaped lump in my belly had somehow disappeared. The last thing in the world I was expecting to see when I peeked from under the duvet was Grandma strolling in with . . . the witch from the gingerbread house!

I howled and screamed and pulled the duvet over me again. 'Don't let her eat me, Grandma, please – I'm sorry, I'm sorry . . . I'll be good from now on, I promise . . .'

'No one's going to eat you, dear,' said Grandma calmly.

I peeked out again.

'What am I still doing here?' I asked, suspiciously.

'Well, dear, you've been very unwell. The doctor here thought it best not to move you.'

'Doctor?'

I noticed the witch had a bag with her. She

placed it on the table, then pulled something from it.

'I'll need some boiling water,' she said to Grandma. Then she made some sort of tea, and placed the cup by the side of the bed. 'How's my patient today?' she said, smiling her still-extremely-scary smile at me.

'You're a *doctor*?' I frowned. 'You mean . . . you're not a witch?'

'Well . . .' she said, waving her hand around vaguely. 'Let's just say I'm a witch doctor and leave it at that, shall we?'

I stared at her in disbelief. 'Wait, did you remove the shoe from my stomach?'

The witch doctor chuckled. 'Just doing my job.'

'So you weren't going to bake me in the oven

when I came to your house then?'

'Of course not! I'd made a roast and you looked so hungry, I thought you'd want to eat it. But before I could take it out, you'd vanished. Now, drink your tea. These herbs will help with your indigestion.'

Well, I didn't know what to believe any more, but the tea smelled good, so I did what I was told.

I had almost finished it when who should swan in but Little Red herself. Oh, the shame! I couldn't even look at her.

'Hey, wolfy,' she said, walking over to the bed.

I put the cup down and shot under the duvet again.

'How's he doing?' I heard her whisper. 'Can he eat yet?'

'A little food would be good, yes,' said the witch.

'I am here you know,' I grumbled from under the duvet. 'You don't have to whisper about me.'

I felt Little Red sit down on the bed. I could smell something good. I poked my head out. She had a basket with her.

'I thought you might be hungry,' she said, 'so I've brought you some pies. Before you get excited, there's still no meat in them – sorry – but the pastry is incredible. Buttery and crumbly and *so* delicious. Honestly, wolfy, you should try one. I really think you might like them.'

Well, I wanted to say no, but my mouth had other ideas. It was hanging open and my tongue was lolling out, slavering all over the bed . . . How long had it been since my last meal? I decided on

balance to swallow my pride – AND a pie. *Whole.* Yup, I sank that baby in one.

'Easy now,' said the witch. 'No wonder you're having tummy trouble! Didn't anyone teach you to chew?'

I shrugged as Little Red offered me another.

'She's right,' said Little Red. 'Break it up with your teeth . . . Things taste much better that way.'

Well, I'll try anything once. I decided to give it a go and eat this one more slowly. I was amazed. Let me tell you – things taste WAY better when you chew! You get the full flavour, know what I mean? Not just a lump in your stomach that tells you you're full, but the herbs, the butter, the delicious, dripping, melty cheese – mmm mmm

MMMMMM — it was *incredible!*

'Good?' asked Little Red.

'Not bad,' I said, trying to play it cool as I reached for a third pie.

'Okay, but that's your last one!' said the witch. 'It's important to know when you're full too.'

'Oh, I almost forgot,' said Little Red, 'you have some visitors outside, if you're up to it?'

I blinked. Visitors? Who would come and visit

the Big Bad Wolf? 'Sure, why not,' I said. I was curious to see who was out there.

When they poked their little heads round the door, I couldn't believe my eyes. They shuffled into the room, hats in their hands, eyes on the floor, tails drooping.

'We're sorry, wolf,' said the first.

'We didn't mean to tease you . . .' said the second.

'Hope we can be friends?' said the third.

Friends? Well, I didn't even know what to say to that. Those little piggies want to be friends with the Big Bad Wolf? You have to respect that sort of bravery!

'Sure, why not?' I said, and in spite of myself, I found I was smiling. 'And, you know, sorry about the whole –' I waved my paw around –

'trying-to-EAT-you thing.'

The pigs laughed nervously, and moved closer to each other.

'Well, that's lovely,' said Little Red, offering pies around to everyone. 'You see, wolfy, vegetables can be just as satisfying as meat.'

Then there was another knock at the door.

'What is this, a birthday party?' I said, but in truth I was enjoying myself now.

'It's open!' called Grandma, and a moment later, a little head popped round the door.

A *wolf's* head!

It was Squirt!

The runtiest wolf from the spring barbecue.

'Hi, Lawrence,' he said in a quiet voice. 'I, um, heard you weren't well and I just came to see how you were doing?'

I opened my mouth, and closed it again, but no words came out. I was in shock. I guess I didn't expect to see any of the pack again after my humiliation at the barbecue, and least of all Squirt. I had been so rude to him.

I wiped at my cheek. I must have got a bit of pastry crust in my eye or something, because I seemed to have tears rolling down my cheek. 'You . . . came to see me? After how I treated you . . .'

I hung my head. I couldn't even finish my sentence.

'It's okay,' he said. 'I knew you didn't mean it.'

Then he turned to Little Red. 'Did you like the new batch?' he asked.

'Oh yes,' she said, beaming. 'These ones are REALLY good! What's the new ingredient?'

'Wild oregano,' he said. 'Found some growing in the woods . . . Seems to really bring out the flavour of the cheese.'

'Wait a minute. Are you telling me YOU made these pies?'

'Yup,' said Squirt. 'I tried to offer you one at the barbecue, but . . .'

'I *told* you that weeks ago, wolfy, but you just ignored me,' Little Red said, sighing.

'These are tasty pies, Squirt,' I said. 'You don't even miss the meat, they're so full of flavour.'

He smiled. 'Thanks, Lawrence.'

'Wait a second –' my mind was working overtime now – 'have you ever tried selling these?'

He shook his head.

'And have you ever tried using . . . what are those things called . . .

MUSHROOMS?'

Monday 1 May

Seventy-five star jumps

Seventy-five press-ups

Seventy-five pull-ups

Well – what a time to be alive! Summer is well and truly in the air today! The sun is warm, the sky is blue and – let me tell you – generally speaking, things are ON THE UP!

'Good morning, Mister Bird!' I said to my friend in the tree who

TWEET-
TWEET-
TWEETED

me out of my bed this morning, as usual. 'And thank you for waking me. You're right — I DO need an early start today.'

Aced my workout too. I am in fine form now, fit as a fiddle and ready for anything!

So once I'd filled my basket with the latest batch of mushrooms from outside my den, I set off for the clearing. When I got there, Wolfman and his crew were still half asleep, lazing around in the shade of the trees.

'Oh great,' muttered Wolfman, 'Lawrence is here . . .' And the others all sniggered, as usual.

'Well, top of the morning to you too, Wolfman! Now, please –' I held up my paw – 'don't get up! I'm afraid I can't stop. Just came to drop off this shipment of wild organic mushrooms, and to collect the brains of the bunch . . . Let me tell you, this guy –' I pointed a thumb in Squirt's direction – 'he may not be the biggest wolf in the pack, but he is huge in the skills department. His pies are going to be Big Bad Business too! You ready over there, Spice Dog?'

Spice Dog – the wolf previously known as Squirt – grinned as he took the mushrooms from me, then handed me a couple of baskets, each one stacked high with delicious-smelling cheese and mushroom pies . . .

'Anyway, can't stop . . . Catch you later, LOSERS!'

And with the pack staring slack-jawed after us, we strolled on out of there, heading for market.

I'll admit, I was a little nervous when we got to the bridge and my old enemy the troll shuffled out in front of us.

'BRIDGE TAX,' he muttered.

But this time I was ready for him.

'Good day to you, Mister Troll, Sir!' I said. 'Now, I don't know about *tax* exactly, but might I interest you in one of these here TASTY AS ANYTHING pies, and don't even think about reaching for that wallet, because we won't accept a penny from you . . . This one's *gratis*, by which I mean, on the house, free, your money is no good here, my trollish friend!' And before he could say anything, I chucked a pie at him and we marched straight past.

We hadn't made it far when he shouted, 'Hey!'

Oh here we go . . . I thought, steeling myself for another dip in the river, but then through a mouthful of pie he cooed, 'This is absolutely delicious! Are those mushrooms in there?'

Or words to that effect – it was hard to tell with his mouth full – but me and Spice Dog took it as a good sign, anyhow.

And indeed the day was a BIG success.

The three little pigs had used their connections at the market to get us one of the best stalls there, and Little Red had even made a banner for us.

'Ta-da!' she said when we arrived. 'What do you think?'

The banner read:

WOLF BROS BIG BAD PIES

Well, Spice Dog and I were speechless.

'Thanks, Red,' I said, at last. 'It's perfection.'

'You're welcome, wolfy,' she said, reaching up to give me a little scratch behind the ear. 'I'm proud of you.'

I have to admit – I do like a little scratch behind the ear. Who knew?

What's more, I'm pleased to report that the new

recipe mushroom pies were a HUGE hit. The stall was a complete sell-out and we had some seriously stiff competition. Rapunzel was selling some phenomenal herbal teas. The witch doctor was there, selling packets of gingerbread, and there was an *enormous* queue outside the golden egg stall. But we held our own, and even had a royal visit – Prince Charming himself stopped by! – and after he'd tried one of the pies, he ordered a whole shipment to the castle!

In no time at all, our baskets were empty and our pockets were full of cold, hard cash. I knew just what to spend it on . . .

'Hello, my good man!' I said, swinging by my favourite stall. 'A string of your finest sausages, please!'

Well, come on, what do you expect? Nobody's perfect. I'm still a wolf after all . . . And, boy, those sausages tasted good! The best I ever had. Responsibly farmed too. It said so on the label.

'Spice Dog . . .' I said, throwing my arm around my new wolfy pal as the sun went down and we made our way back over the bridge towards the woods. 'How about we start our own pack?'

'You got it, L-Man!'

I still had one pie left, and I broke it in two, handing him a chunk.

'For the road!'

We both grinned and took a giant bite, savouring those juicy flavours. Then we threw back our heads and . . .

Meet Everyone in the

Fairytale Woods

Lawrence

That's me! The BIG BAD WOLF. Also, the smartest, fastest, most charming and handsome wolf in the Fairytale Woods.

Little Red

A little girl in a bright red cape who visits her Grandmother every Sunday. How sweet! NO! Don't let her fool you . . . Little Red is rude, sneaky and ANNOYING.

TASTINESS LEVEL: OFF THE SCALE

The Three Little Pigs

There's nothing more annoying than a giggling pig . . . except THREE giggling pigs! What do they have to be so happy about?

TASTINESS LEVEL: THREE FOR THE PRICE OF ONE

The Troll

The grumpiest creature in the Fairytale Woods. Takes his job as bridge tax collector waaay too seriously.

TASTINESS LEVEL: TOO CRANKY.

The Witch

A very scary old woman. Lives in a house made entirely of gingerbread – strange, but delicious.

TASTINESS LEVEL: TOO WARTY.

The Woodcutter

The only HELPFUL person in all of the Fairytale Woods, but also the most gullible. Makes a great soup.

TASTINESS LEVEL: TOO DOPEY.

Grandma

Old and sweet, but pretty speedy. Wears a size medium (like me).

TASTINESS LEVEL: MATURE.

WRITE YOUR OWN FAIRYTALE DIARY!

What do you think the people of the Fairytale Woods get up to when we're not there? Maybe the Three Bears love to experiment with porridge flavours. Perhaps someone has hidden Prince Charming's *favourite* jumper and there's trouble brewing in the Fairytale Castle. We've heard that Sleeping Beauty is having trouble nodding off . . .

It's over to you now. Tell us *your* favourite fairytale as a diary. Turn the page, share the adventure!

BEN MILLER is the bestselling author
of magical stories for all the family:
The Night I Met Father Christmas,
The Boy Who Made the World Disappear,
The Day I Fell Into a Fairytale,
How I Became a Dog Called Midnight,
The Night We Got Stuck in a Story,
Once Upon a Legend,
Diary of a Christmas Elf,
Secrets of a Christmas Elf,
Adventures of a Christmas Elf.

He is an actor, director and comedian, best-known for the
Armstrong and Miller sketch show, the Johnny English and
Paddington films, BBC's Death in Paradise and
Netflix smash, Bridgerton.

 @actualbenmiller

BEN MILLER
TURN THE PAGE,
share the Adventure

THE Magical BLOCKBUSTER FROM
BEN MILLER

TURN THE PAGE, share the Adventure

ONCE UPON A LEGEND

Illustrations by Elisa Paganelli